This book belongs to:

....

....

Retold by Monica Hughes
Illustrated by Daniel Howarth

Reading consultants: Betty Root and Monica Hughes

Marks and Spencer p.l.c.
PO Box 3339
Chester, CH99 9QS

shop online
www.marksandspencer.com

ISBN 1-84461-815-3
Printed in China

First Readers

Rumpelstiltskin

MARKS &
SPENCER

Helping your child to read

First Readers are closely linked to the National Curriculum. Their vocabulary has been carefully selected from the word lists recommended by the National Literacy Strategy.

Read the story

Read the story to your child a few times.

The miller's daughter began to cry. Then she saw the little man. "What will you give me if I help you" he said. "I will give you my ring," she said.

Follow your finger

Run your finger under the text as you read. Your child will soon begin to follow the words with you.

Look at the pictures

Talk about the pictures. They will help your child to understand the story.

"What will you give me?"

17

Have a go

Let your child have a go at reading the large type on each right-hand page. It repeats a line from the story.

Join in

When your child is ready, encourage them to join in with the main story text. Shared reading is the first step to reading alone.

Once upon a time there was a miller.
The miller had a daughter.
One day the king rode by.
"My daughter can spin straw into
gold," the miller told the king.

The miller had a daughter.

So the king took the miller's
daughter to his castle.
He took her to a room full of straw.
"Spin this straw into gold," said
the king.
Then he left her alone all night.

"Spin this straw into gold."

The miller's daughter could not spin
straw into gold.
She began to cry.
But then she saw a little man.
"I can spin straw into gold," he said.
"What will you give me if I help you?"
"I will give you my necklace," said the
miller's daughter.

She saw a little man.

In the morning the little man had gone and the room was full of gold.

The king came to see the miller's daughter.
He was very pleased.
The king took her to a big room.
The room was full of straw.
"Spin this straw into gold," said the king.
Then he left her alone all night.

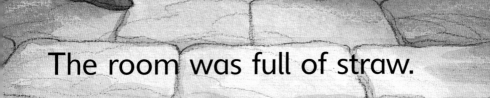
The room was full of straw.

15

The miller's daughter began to cry.
Then she saw the little man.
"What will you give me if I help you?"
he said.
"I will give you my ring," she said.

16

"What will you give me?"

In the morning the little man had gone and the room was full of gold.

The king came to see the miller's daughter.
He was very pleased.
The king took the miller's daughter to a bigger room full of straw.
"Spin this straw into gold and I will marry you," said the king.
Then he left her alone all night.

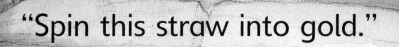

"Spin this straw into gold."

The miller's daughter began to cry.
Then she saw the little man.
"What will you give me if I help you?"
he said.
"I have nothing to give you," she said.
"I will help you again," said the little
man, "but you must give me your first
baby."

"I have nothing to give you."

21

In the morning the little man had gone and the room was full of gold.

The king married the miller's daughter.

Soon the queen had a baby.

She forgot all about the little man.

One day the little man came to take the baby.

The queen began to cry.

"I will not take your baby if you can guess my name," he said. "I will come back in the morning."

The queen had a baby.

That night the queen went for a walk
in the woods.
She tried to guess the little man's name.
"Is it Don or Ron?" she said to herself.
"Is it Bill or Will?"
Then the queen saw the little man.
He was dancing round a fire singing,

"My name is Rumpelstiltskin.
Rumpelstiltskin is my name."

The queen saw the little man.

In the morning the little man came to see the queen.

"Is your name Don or Ron?" said the queen.

"No! No! No!" said the little man.

"Is your name Bill or Will?" said the queen.

"No! No! No!" said the little man.

Then the queen said, "Is your name Rumpelstiltskin?"

"Yes! Yes! Yes!" said the little man and off he ran.

And they never saw Rumpelstiltskin again.

They never saw
Rumpelstiltskin again.

Look back in your book.
Can you read these words?

daughter

king

little man

straw

gold

Can you answer these questions?

Who asked the miller's daughter to spin straw into gold?

What did the miller's daughter give to the little man?

What was the little man's name?

First Readers

(subject to availability)

Beauty and the Beast
Chicken Licken
Cinderella
The Elves and the Shoemaker
The Enormous Turnip
The Gingerbread Man
Goldilocks and the Three Bears
Hansel and Gretel
Jack and the Beanstalk
Little Red Riding Hood
The Princess and the Pea
Rapunzel
Rumpelstiltskin
Sleeping Beauty
Snow White and the Seven Dwarfs
The Three Billy Goats Gruff
The Three Little Pigs
The Ugly Duckling